Once Upon a Farm

by Marie Bradby

illustrated by Ted Rand

Orchard Books / New York

An Imprint of Scholastic Inc.

Library of Congress Cataloging-in-Publication Data
Bradby, Marie.
Once upon a farm / by Marie Bradby ; illustrated by Ted Rand.—lst ed.
p. cm.
Summary: Illustrations and simple rhyming text recall life on a family farm.
ISBN 0-439-31766-5 (alk. paper)
[1. Farm life—Fiction. 2. Stories in rhyme.] I. Rand, Ted, ill. II. Title.
PZ8.3.B7265 On   2002 [E]—dc21   2001-032935

10 9 8 7 6 5 4 3 2 1   02 03 04 05

Printed in Singapore   46
First edition, March 2002
Book design by Mina Greenstein
The text of this book is set in 16 point New Baskerville.
The illustrations are watercolor.

To all family farmers, especially ours—
Steve and Karen Smith of Ewingsford Farm,
Community Supported Agriculture (CSA)

—M.B.

To my daughter, Theresa, the family farmer

—T.R.

Amule
a tiller
work till dinner.

A stump
a rock
pull till you drop.

I hold Mama's hand,
Daddy carries Sue.
We see rabbits, deer, and shooting stars when work is through.

A dip
a dell
dig a sweet well.

A saw
some wood
the new home stood.

I rode the banister,
landed on the floor.
If Sue hadn't stopped me, I would've sailed out the door.

A plow
some grain
pray for rain.

A sow
a shed
may all be fed.

Mama cooks the corn cakes,
Daddy says the prayer.
Sorghum, ham, and jelly—it's been a good year.

A nanny
a hen
corn in the bin.

A wrench
good luck
fixed the truck.

Sue grooms her pony,
I muck the stalls.
We might win a ribbon at the state fair after all.

A dove
a ring
wake up and sing.

A hawk
the sky
riding currents high.

Daddy drives the combine.
We ride along.
I hope we never leave this place—especially the swim pond.

A nest
a toad
chicks in the road.

A flower
a bee
old apple tree.

Mama gave us baskets,
said, "Go out there and pick."
We ate green apples, worms and all, and were we ever sick!

A clover
a field
cow's daily meal.

A pail
a light
milk day and night.

I cranked the churn
till my arm was sore.
Thought of Mama's ice cream and cake, then cranked it some more.

A barn
a bale
tell a tall tale.

A fence
a row
tractor to mow.

When I chased the goat
he butted my backside.
I jumped the fence, tore my pants, and Sue laughed till she cried.

A highway
a light
flashing in the night.

A mall
a town
been spreading round.

In the quiet woods
where the stream ran,
we built castles out of sticks and sailed boats to foreign lands.

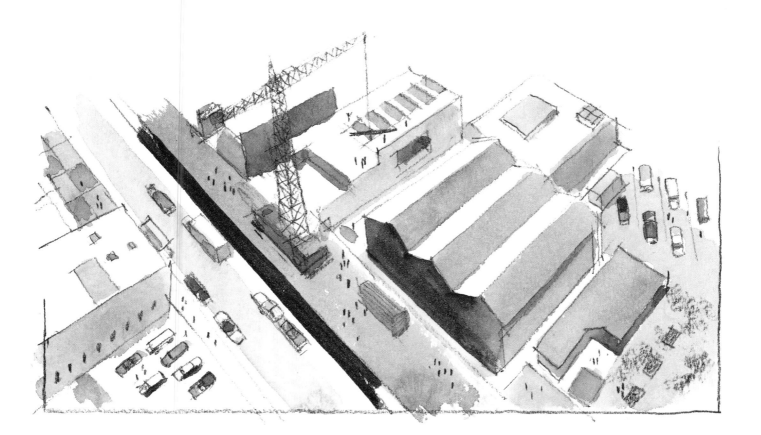

A beetle

a fly

a cow gone dry.

A rabbit

a farm

they're all gone.

There was a secret place
high in the oak tree
where I could sit and think about what I was going to be.

A bulldozer
a crane
new buildings on Main.

A sale
a sign
move with the times.

I took a heart full—
things we didn't sell—
how a stream sounds, the way rain clouds look, how sweet dirt smells.